THE QUOTATIONS OF

J.R. EWING

Memorable dialogue from the CBS-TV series "Dallas," Created by David Jacobs – a Lorimar® Production

Selected from scripts written by:
> Camille Marchetta
> Rena Down
> Lorraine Despres
> Arthur Bernard Lewis
> Leonard Katzman
> Barbara Searles
> Worley Thorne
> Darlene Craviotto
> Linda B. Elstad
> David Michael Jacobs & Arthur Bernard Lewis
> Jeff Young

Edited by
Diane J. Perlberg & Joelle Delbourgo

BANTAM BOOKS
Toronto / New York / London

THE QUOTATIONS OF J.R. EWING

A Bantam Book/OCTOBER 1980

ISBN 0-553-14440-5

Published simultaneously in the United States and Canada

Bantam Books are published by Bantam Books, Inc. Its trademark, consisting of the words "Bantam Books" and the por-
trayal of a bantam, is Registered in U.S. Patent and Trademark
Office and in other countries. Marca Registrada. Bantam
Books, Inc., 666 Fifth Avenue, New York, New York 10103.

PRINTED IN THE UNITED STATES OF AMERICA

0 9 8 7 6 5 4 3 2 1

"I may just keep you around, Kristin, if you can pick up your typing speed."

ON THE IMPORTANCE
OF THE SABBATH

"It wasn't Sunday School I came here for."

LIVING WELL IS *STILL* THE BEST REVENGE

ON THE IMPORTANCE
OF THE NUCLEAR FAMILY

"However I spend my playtime I never forget
my first loyalty is to my family, my wife and
my child."

ON THE IMPORTANCE OF A DRINKING BUDDY

"I'm kind of particular who I drink with."

ON HOUSEKEEPING

"If I had time to clear up the mess, I'd shoot you."

"Smart girl like you. I wouldn't be surprised if you started to diversify your asset. Sort of create a hedge against sudden devaluation."

Bobby: "I'm still your brother."
J.R.: "My brother? As far as I'm concerned, I'm an only child."

"You'll see, Mama. You'll be proud of me yet."

ON HOW TO HANDLE ONE'S WIFE

"If she were my wife, I'd kick her tail to Austin and back."

ON THE EWING BRAND OF HOSPITALITY

"When my daddy entertains, he goes all out. That's what the Ewings are all about. Doing big things in a big way."

"...A cardinal rule of politics — never get caught in bed with a live man or a dead woman."

"I never steered you wrong before."

"I know I've given you a hard time in the past..."

"I'm going to try to make you happy to be here."

UNDERSTATEMENT OF THE YEAR

Sue Ellen: "I would say that our life together
leaves something
to be desired, wouldn't you?"
J.R.: "Nothing's perfect, Sue Ellen."

"You better practice up on your tall tales. You can fool your grandparents with a kiss but not your Uncle J.R. I know a lie when I hear one..."

IGNORANT SLUT SELECTION

"She's dirt—which she manages to cover with some good clothes and some style. But the dirt's still there. Everyone can see it."

Sue Ellen: "You've already ruined his career.

ON MANKIND

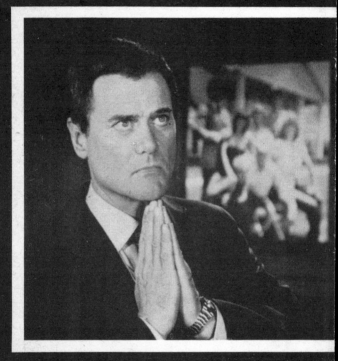

"Every man has his weakness."

IGNORANT SLUT SELECTION

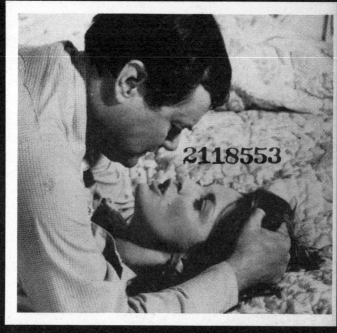

2118553

J.R.: "Do you know you smile in your sleep?"
Sue Ellen: "Do I?"
J.R.: "Tramp!"

IGNORANT SLUT SELECTION

"Anyone can see she's cracking slowly and surely. But who could blame her? Her 'dear daddy' no relation to her at all. Her real father a saddle tramp and a thief. Her mother, a whore...."

IGNORANT SLUT SELECTION

"Go on, prove to everyone you're Valene's daughter, a scheming, blackmailing little tramp."

J.R. SENDS HIS REGRETS...

"The only thing I'm ever gonna be sorry about is it wasn't you instead of Julie who fell off that roof."

"I admire a man with a little spunk."

"I'm a married man. I believe in the sanctity of marriage."

YET MORE FAMOUS LAST WORDS

"The honeymoon appears to be over."

"You just better get used to what is. 'Cause I'm sure not changin'."

EVEN MORE FAMOUS LAST WORDS

"My daddy and I would never do anything illegal."

"I could be a faithful husband and loving father if you gave me the chance."

ON HUMAN AFFECTION

ON FAMILY SKELETONS

Jock: "There's bound to be a body in that closet. Find it."

J.R.: "Yes, daddy. I'll either find it — or put it there."

Jock: "Just keep spreadin the B's."
J.R.: "Yes, sir, booty, booze and broads ..."

Cliff Barnes: "I guess not even you are capable
of cold blooded murder."
J.R.: "That was before I found out about your
cheap little romance with my wife."

ON HOW TO LOSE GRACEFULLY

"It's just amazing to me that you're not a better loser, Cliff. After all, you have had a lot of practice."

"I want to see you smile at me the way you did at that cowboy."

"Haven't you noticed it takes a man to play in my league? (Now run along. I'm busy").

ON APPROPRIATE FINANCIAL COMPENSATION

"You can walk the streets before I'll ever give you a dime."

Kristin: "You want me to sell myself so I can spy
on your friends. Is that it?"
J.R.: "You're always saying you want to help."

ON FLATTERING ONE'S COMPANION

Sue Ellen: "Tell me J.R., which slut are you staying with tonight?"

J.R.: "Does it matter? Whoever it is, she'll be more interesting than the slut I'm looking at right now."

ON OVERCOMING
INTERNATIONAL BARRIERS

"Money speaks all languages."

ON HOW ONE CAN BEST GROW IN J.R.'s GARDEN

Kristin: "Familiarity breeds contempt, is that what you're saying?"

J.R.: "Oh, I wouldn't say 'contempt' exactly... But it *does* take some of the bloom off the rose, don't you think?"

THE EWINGS OF DALLAS

The Ewings of Dallas—the most closely watched family of America. Now, you can follow TV's most fascinating family in these three new titles from Bantam. You'll want to complete your own set and order additional copies as gifts for fellow Dallas addicts.

THE DALLAS FAMILY ALBUM   (01289-4) $6.95

This large format (8⅜"x10⅞") book contains over 150 photographs (many in color), narrative captions, and star biographies which bring the illustrious Ewing family to life.

THE EWINGS OF DALLAS   (14439-1) $2.75
Burt Hirschfeld

Follow the escapades of the Ewings—the oil barons of Texas who love, hate, and wheel and deal their way to fortune.

THE QUOTATIONS OF J.R. EWING   (14440-5) $1.50

The pithy sayings of America's favorite villain. "Not since John Milton gave Satan all the good lines in *Paradise Lost* has a villain so appalled—and fascinated—the world."—*People Magazine*